It's time for an ADVENTURE,

goggi-geeha ...

EGMONT
We bring stories to life

First published in Great Britain 2012 by Egmont UK Limited
239 Kensington High Street, London W8 6SA

Baby Jake characters and logo © Darrall Macqueen Limited
2012. Baby Jake is a trademark of Darrall Macqueen
Limited. Licensed by BBC Worldwide Limited.
BBC logo TM & © BBC 1996. All rights reserved.

ISBN 978 1 4052 6366 5
51919/1
Printed in Italy

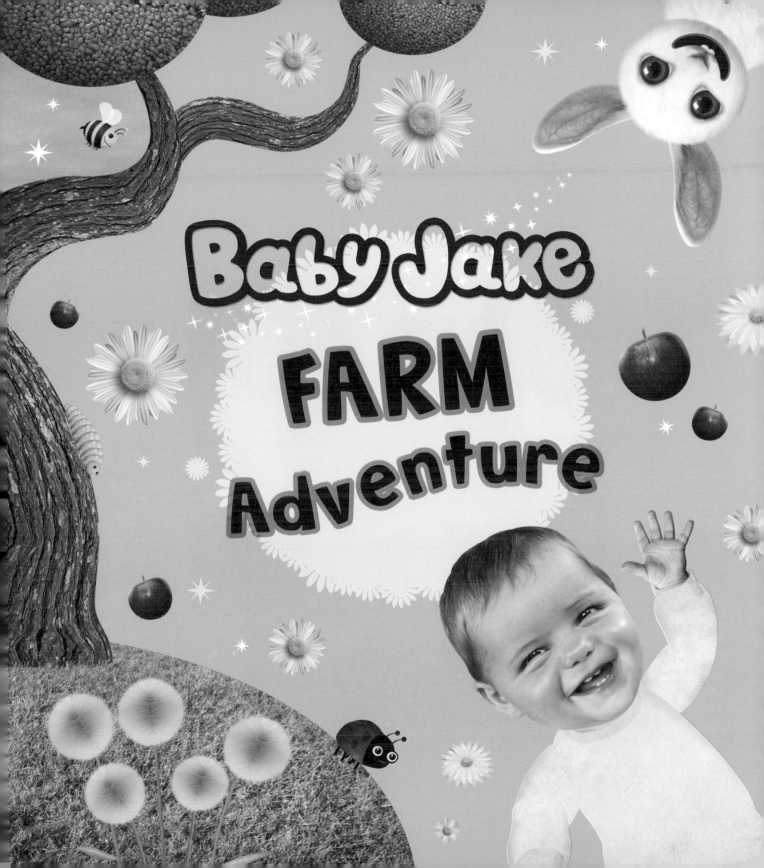

Baby Jake

FARM Adventure

Toot! Toot!

It's Toot Toot the Tractor!

It's going to be a **farm** adventure!

Hello Jakey!

Look, there are bouncy apples everywhere!

Boing! Boing!

Who is that?

Yes, it's **Nibbles** the rabbit.

Hello, **Nibbles!**

Baby Jake and Nibbles are bouncing

like bouncy apples.

Baby Jake bounces **up** and **down**.

Oh no, the apple is bouncing into the rabbit hole.

Look!

Find that bouncy apple Baby Jake.

Well done!

You are a boingy, bouncy,

magic baby, Jakey!

Hooray!
Let's sing!

Yacki, yacki, yoggi
with the HAMSTERNAUTS ...

Flappy, clappy fun with
NIBBLES of course ...

Yacki, yacki, yoggi,
let's do it **again!**

Yacki, yacki, yoggi – doo, doo, dee.
Yacki, yacki, yoggi, beep beep – noo see!
Bah, bah, bah, beep beep – noo see!
Yacki, yacki, yoggi – moo moo moo.
That's just what we love to do!

Yacki, yacki, yoggi – doo, doo, dee.
Bah, bah, bah, beep beep – noo see!
Yacki, yacki, yoggi – moo moo moo.
Hope you love to do it too!

What is it, Baby Jake?

What can you see now?

Yes! It's a wriggly **caterpillar!**

Baby Jake loves to tummy wriggle.

Nibbles loves to tummy wriggle, too.

What a wriggly, giggly pair!

wriggle

wriggle

It's getting very **Windy,** Jakey!

Look at all the dandelion clocks flying in the air.

Oh no!

You're not going to, are you Baby Jake?

Chase!

You are! Baby Jake!

You're flying higher and higher and higher.

You're flying all the way home!

Bye bye Toot Toot.

Bye bye Nibbles.

Bye bye apples.

Bye bye wriggly caterpillar.

Goodbye!

Baby Jake and me,

Baby Jake and you,

We've had a MAGIC time today ...

Dee zee dee see doo!